This Little Hippo
book belongs to

_____

_____

Scholastic Children's Books,
Commonwealth House, 1-19 New Oxford Street,
London WC1A 1NU, UK
a division of Scholastic Ltd

London ~ New York ~ Toronto ~ Sydney ~ Auckland

First published by Scholastic Ltd, 1998

Developed from the original book The Night After Christmas,
by James Stephenson. The Forgotten Toys is an animated series produced
by Hibbert Ralph Entertainment for Link Entertainment,
scripted by Mark Holloway,
directed by Graham Ralph and produced by Karen Davidsen.
Executive producers: David Hamilton and Claire Derry.
Script adaptation by Norman Redfern. Book illustrations by Maureen Galvani.
All rights reserved.

2 4 6 8 10 9 7 5 3 1

ISBN 0 590 19968 4

Printed in Belgium

The Forgotten Toys

New Zoo

Little Hippo

Once upon a time, when they were far away from home,
a little girl and her brother lost their favourite toys . . . and the
toys didn't like being lost. Now Teddy, and Annie the ragdoll,
were on their way home, but the journey back to their children
was long and full of adventures.

One day, they stopped outside a zoo.

"I want to see the bears," said Teddy. "They're family."

"You're not a bear," said Annie. "You're a teddy."

"No, I'm a bear called Teddy," insisted Teddy. "Are you coming?"

As they looked around the zoo, Annie and Teddy realised that something was wrong. All the animals were miserable. Even the hyena was too sad to laugh.

Teddy spotted the bears.

"Oi! Cousins!" he shouted. "I'm a bear, just like you."

The bears just turned away.

"Let's go," sighed Teddy.

"No, we can't," said Annie. "Something terrible is happening here."

An old elephant was standing nearby. His trunk had a knot in it.

"Excuse me," Annie asked him, "why are all the animals so sad?"

"I can't remember," replied the elephant.

"But elephants never forget," Annie reminded him.

"Don't they?" asked the elephant. "I've got a memory like a sieve. I tied a knot in my trunk to remind me to . . . I've forgotten what it was! Ask the Thingy. He's over there."

Teddy and Annie weren't sure what kind of animal the Thingy was. But they were sure that he was a very sad Thingy.

"What's wrong?" Annie asked.

"She's leaving us," sobbed the Thingy. "Climb aboard and I'll show you."

Annie and Teddy climbed on to the Thingy's back and rode round to the zoo gates. A lady with a battered suitcase was trudging away down the road.

"That's her," said the Thingy. "The kindest, best zoo-keeper ever, and she's leaving."

The zoo-keeper turned and waved to the Thingy, who burst into tears again.

"She spent all her money looking after us," sobbed the Thingy. "Now there's none left and she's had to sell the zoo."

"I'm sure the new zoo-keeper will be just as nice," said Annie.

"No, he won't," said the Thingy.

The new zoo-keeper was already at work. Teddy, Annie and the Thingy watched him inspecting the animals.

"You've been using far too much toothpaste," he snapped at the crocodiles.

"And you," he told the ostrich, "will have to wear the same size scarf as everyone else!"

"I just told you; no second helpings!" he reminded the forgetful elephant. "You're on a diet!"

Next, it was the Thingy's turn. Annie and Teddy hid.

"What on earth are you?" inquired the keeper. "No-one's going to pay to see you. You'll be the first to go!"

"Poor animals," whispered Annie. "We've got to help them."

Late that night, the animals all gathered together for a special meeting. Teddy told them his plan.

"The new zoo-keeper gets his money from all the visitors to the zoo," he explained. "All you have to do is stop the visitors coming, then there won't be any money and he won't be a zoo-keeper any more."

Next morning, the new keeper opened the gates and eagerly showed his first customers around. Teddy and Annie raced to tip off their friends.

"They're on their way!" called Teddy.

"Monkeys first!" said Annie.

"My zoo has the funniest monkeys in the world!" boasted the zoo-keeper.

The visitors weren't convinced. The monkey house looked more like a library. Monkeys wearing reading glasses sat in silence, their noses buried in books.

"Is that all they do?" asked a customer.

"No," said the keeper. "They can swing from the trees, peel bananas with their feet . . ."

"Ssshhhh!" hissed the monkeys.

"Come and see the zebras," whispered the zoo-keeper. Teddy and Annie were busy with paint pots and brushes. They finished just in time.

"If those are zebras," complained a customer, "where are their stripes?"

"Er . . . come and see the lions," said the keeper. "They are truly the most ferocious you will ever see!"

The visitors clustered around the lions' cage and peered inside. The lions didn't look very dangerous. Some of them were dancing to pop music, and one was pushing a pram full of little baby rabbits.

"Very ferocious! I'm so scared!" laughed one of the customers.
"Well, I want my money back," said another.
"Me too!"

On their way out, all the visitors insisted on having their money back. The animals cheered, but the new zoo-keeper was furious. He stomped back to the middle of the zoo.

"There is a new zoo rule," he told the animals. "No visitors – no food!"

Then he stormed out and slammed the gates behind him.

"What are we going to do now?" asked the Thingy.

"I don't know," replied Annie.

By night-time, the animals were starving. They gathered dejectedly in the middle of the zoo for another meeting.

"Listen," cried Teddy. "You don't have to put up with this. You could find someone else to look after you."

"We could go back to our old keeper," suggested the Thingy.

"Yeah, why not?" said Teddy. "We'll take them, won't we, Pigtails?"

While the people of the city were asleep in their beds, the animals made their way through the silent streets. They stopped outside a little house. Annie climbed on to the elephant's head and knocked on the bedroom window.

"What are you doing up here?" asked the old zoo-keeper.

"Look who's come to see you!" said Annie.

"Come in," said the lady. "Come in!"

The animals made themselves at home in their friend's little house. There were crocodiles in the bath, bears under the stairs; soon every nook-and-cranny seemed to have a furry creature in it. The old zoo-keeper was delighted to see them, but after feeding them all, she sat down with a sigh.

"What's wrong?" asked Annie.

"It's lovely to see them again," said the lady, "but they can't stay. This isn't a zoo."

"It could be," said Teddy. "If you wanted it to be."

"But my house is far too small to be a zoo," argued the lady.

"That's it!" exclaimed Teddy. "It's going to be the smallest zoo in the world!"

"And the animals will help," said Annie. "Won't you?"

Suddenly the room was filled with smiling, nodding animals, all eager to help. The monkeys raced around the city, handing out leaflets for the world's smallest zoo. By the time the doors opened, there was a queue of excited customers waiting outside.

They paid for their tickets and began to explore the zoo. Behind one door, they found a pride of ferocious lions. Behind another, a pack of playful bears. And then there was the Thingy. They weren't sure what he was, but they were sure that they liked him.

After tea with the penguins, the visitors went home, delighted with their day at the zoo.

The old zoo-keeper finished counting her money and popped it into the kangaroo's pouch for safe-keeping.

"We never had so many visitors at the old zoo," she told Annie and Teddy. "My animals can stay here for ever. Will you stay, too?"

"We'd like to," said Annie, "but we can't."

"We've got to find our way home," explained Teddy.

Annie and Teddy waved goodbye to their friends.

"You know what's wrong with that zoo?" Teddy said as they walked away. "The bears. They don't look like me."

And the forgotten toys set off again in search of their family.